MEG and MOG

for Loveday

MEG and MOG

by Helen Nicoll
and Jan Pieńkowski

PUFFIN BOOKS

Once upon a time
there was a witch
called Meg

At midnight
the owl hooted 3 times
and woke her up

She got out of bed
to dress for
the spell party

She
put
on

her black
stockings

her big
black shoes

her long
black cloak

and her tall
black hat

She went down the stairs to cook breakfast

CLIP CLOP

In the kitchen
lay her big
striped cat Mog
He was
fast asleep

She trod on Mog's tail

She put it all
in her cauldron
and stirred it up

BUBBLE BUBBLE

At 1 o'clock
she got
her broomstick
her cauldron
and
a spider

and
she
flew
up
the
chimney
with
Mog

Up in the sky

she met her friends
going to the party
Bess

Jess

Tess

and

Cress

They landed on a hill
in the moonlight
to make the spell

Each of them
had brought something
to put in the cauldron

There was
a flash
and a bang

BOOM

Something had gone wrong

Bess, Jess,
Tess and Cress
all changed into mice
and Mog chased them

Goodbye!